MONSTERS
UNIVERSITY

ADAPTED BY BARBARA BAZALDUA
ILLUSTRATED BY THE DISNEY STORYBOOK ARTISTS

A GOLDEN BOOK • NEW YORK

ISBN 978-0-7364-3043-2
randomhouse.com/kids
Printed in the United States of America
10 9 8 7 6 5 4 3 2 1

Six-year-old Mike Wazowski was the smallest monster in his first-grade class. He was hardly ever noticed by his classmates. One day, Mike's class went on a field trip to Monsters, Inc., a company that collected the screams of human children to power the monster world.

Mike couldn't contain his excitement. He snuck through a door on a scare floor and watched a Scarer collect screams from a real human child. It was thrilling, dangerous, and awesome—all at the same time. **At that moment, Mike knew he wanted to be a Scarer more than anything in the world!**

Twelve years later, the day came for Mike to attend Monsters University. He gazed in awe at the School of Scaring building. **He knew this was where he belonged!**

As Mike walked past some club booths, a flyer caught his eye. It was for the Scare Games—a competition that determined the scariest monsters on campus. Mike thought the games sounded exciting!

Mike headed to his dorm room to meet his roommate. When he opened the door, **a small lizardlike monster leaped forward**. "The name's Randy Boggs, scaring major," he said, shaking Mike's hand.

"Mike Wazowski, scaring major," replied Mike.

Randy smiled. "I can tell we're going to be best chums."

The next day, Mike attended his first class: Scaring 101. Dean Hardscrabble, the head of the Scaring Program, spoke to the class. As a professional Scarer, Hardscrabble had broken the **all-time scare record**.

She warned the new students: "Fail the final exam at the end of the semester, and you are **out of the Scaring Program**."

The scaring teacher, Professor Knight, began asking the class questions. Mike was the first student to answer, but he was quickly interrupted.

"RAARRRRR!"

The roar shook the room and a huge monster with messy blue fur stumbled in and flopped down in a chair.

"Sullivan. Jimmy Sullivan. You can call me Sulley," he announced.

After class, Mike went back to his room to study. **As he sat at his desk, a critter came flying through his window—followed by Sulley!** Sulley had stolen Archie the Scare Pig, the mascot of rival school Fear Tech. He wanted to impress the Roar Omega Roars, the top fraternity on campus.

When Archie grabbed Mike's prized MU hat and jumped out the window, Mike went right after him!

After a wild chase through campus, Mike trapped Archie in a garbage can. Sulley picked up both Mike and Archie and held them high. “MU rules!” he yelled.

Everyone thought Sulley had captured Archie. The Roar Omega Roars were very impressed.

Mike tried to explain that *he* had actually caught the scare pig, but no one listened to him. The RORs wouldn't even allow him into their party.

"This party is for scare students who actually have a chance," Sulley told Mike.

Mike was steamed. **"I'll scare circles around you this year!"** he shouted.

All semester, Mike holed himself up in the library, practiced his scare techniques, and aced every exam. Meanwhile, Sulley goofed off and barely passed his tests.

Johnny Worthington, the ROR president, was having doubts about Sulley. **If Sulley didn't shape up, he would be kicked out of the fraternity.**

On the day of the final exam, Mike and Sulley got into a roaring face-off. As they lunged at one another, Sulley accidentally stumbled backward. He knocked over and **broke the scream can** that held Dean Hardscrabble's record-breaking scream!

The room fell silent. Hardscrabble descended from the rafters. She picked up her broken scream can.

"You will not be continuing in the Scaring Program," she told Mike and Sulley.

Mike refused to give up his dream of becoming a Scarer. He found the Scare Games flyer in his dorm room and came up with a **brilliant idea**. He ran off to sign up for the games! Mike thought if he could win the Scare Games, it would prove to Hardscrabble that he belonged in the Scaring Program.

To take part in the Scare Games, Mike joined the Oozma Kappa fraternity. Then he made a risky deal with Hardscrabble. **If he and the OKs won the Scare Games, she would let them all into the Scaring Program.** If they lost, Mike would leave Monsters University. But Mike's team needed one more player to qualify. Sulley was the only one to volunteer. Mike was furious, but he had no choice. He had to let Sulley join the team.

When Mike and Sulley arrived at the Oozma Kappa fraternity house, Squishy, Don, Art, Terri, and Terry welcomed them.

The OKs were thrilled to be part of the Scare Games. But there was a problem: the OKs looked cute, cuddly, and extremely friendly. **They were the exact opposite of scary!**

The first event was a race through a dark tunnel filled with **stinging glow urchins**. Mike and Sulley abandoned their teammates and charged ahead.

The RORs finished first. Mike and Sulley finished second, but since they had left their teammates behind, the OKs were eliminated. Luckily, another team was disqualified, so the OKs were put back in the games.

The next day, the OKs wanted to show Mike their "talents." Don said he was stealthy, but his tentacles made loud popping noises. Terri and Terry claimed they were master magicians.

"It's all about misdirection," said Terri.

But their card trick failed miserably.

Mike told the OKs to take all their natural instincts and bury them deep, deep down.

Sulley had seen enough. He wanted to leave the OKs and find another fraternity. But the game rules didn't allow it. **Mike insisted they do things his way from now on.**

Sulley walked off. He thought the OKs were hopeless.

For the next event, each team had to get across the library and grab their flag without getting caught by the librarian.

The OKs slowly crept toward their flag. Then Sulley got impatient. **As he scrambled up a ladder, it broke!** To Mike's surprise, the OKs came to Sulley's rescue. They distracted the librarian, giving the team a chance to escape.

The OKs had made it safely outside, but they didn't have their flag. Mike was devastated! They had failed. **But suddenly, Squishy appeared—holding the flag!**

"How . . . ?" asked Mike.

Terri leaned into Mike. "Misdirection," he said.

For the first time, Mike had a glimmer of hope.

Nearby, Hardscrabble looked on. She couldn't believe the OKs were still in the Scare Games.

The following evening, Mike took the OKs to Monsters, Inc. Gazing down at a scare floor, they saw monsters of all shapes, sizes, and ages.

"There's no one type of Scarer," Mike pointed out. **"The best Scarers use their differences to their advantage."**

All of the OKs were inspired, and Mike and Sulley agreed that they needed to start working together as a team.

From then on, the OKs trained hard. Mike had them practice their roaring and hiding skills. He also had them do push-ups and "scary feet" drills. It didn't take long before **they were ready for the next Scare Games event**!

The OKs worked together and survived the third and fourth events. **That meant they were heading to the finals with the RORs!**

Sulley was sure the OKs would win the Scare Games, but Hardscrabble didn't agree.

"Tomorrow each of you must prove that you are undeniably scary, and **I know for a fact one of you is not**," she told him.

Sulley knew she meant Mike.

Late that night, Sulley coached Mike on his roaring. **"Reach deep down and let the scary out!"** he said.

Mike let out his deepest, loudest roar. Sulley smiled and gave Mike a high five. But as Mike drifted off to sleep, Sulley couldn't help wondering if Hardscrabble was right.

The final Scare Games event took place in the Monsters University amphitheater. The stands were packed with hundreds of cheering fans. They were all there to see the **OKs and the RORs go head to head**.

Each competitor had to perform a scare in a scare simulator, which was set to the highest difficulty level.

One by one, the OKs performed a successful scare and increased the level on the team's scream can. Soon their score was tied with the RORs.

The last two competitors were Johnny Worthington and Mike.

"Don't take the loss too hard," Johnny taunted. "You never belonged here anyway."

Mike was more determined than ever!

Mike entered the simulator, avoided the toys on the floor, ruffled the curtains, and crept alongside the bed. Then he closed his eyes. This was it. He took a deep breath and let out his most explosive roar! The robot child sat bolt upright—and filled the scream can all the way to the top. **The OKs had won the Scare Games!**

The RORs were in a state of shock. They couldn't believe they had just lost to the Oozma Kappas!

As the stadium erupted with cheers, Sulley hoisted Mike up in the air. **"We're in the Scaring Program!"** Sulley shouted. The OKs cried tears of joy.

GO OK
OK

As everyone was leaving, Mike wandered over to the simulator. "Boo!" he said to the robot child. It let out a bloodcurdling scream.

Puzzled, Mike examined the control panel. The simulator had been set on the highest difficulty for every competitor—except Mike. His setting was on easy.

"Did you do this?" Mike asked Sulley.

Sulley hesitated for a moment. "I . . . I . . . Yes, I did. But you don't understand—"

Mike was heartbroken and angry. **"You don't think I'm scary!"** he cried.

Mike stormed away, leaving Sulley and the other OKs behind. They had heard everything, and they were crushed.

Sulley walked through the campus. He spotted Hardscrabble on the School of Scaring steps. He went up to her and confessed everything.

"I expect you off campus by tomorrow," she said.

Just then, **the alarm went off in the door tech lab**. Dean Hardscrabble flew off to investigate. *Oh no,* thought Sulley. *Mike!*

Mike had entered the human world through one of the doors in the lab. He skillfully rolled across the bedroom floor, ruffled the curtains, crept up to the child's bed, and roared.

A little girl sat up and stared at Mike.

"You look funny," she said, smiling at him.

Mike couldn't believe the little girl wasn't scared of him. Suddenly, he heard a sound on the other side of the room and turned around.

To his horror, Mike realized he wasn't in a child's bedroom. **He was in a cabin full of kids!**

Back at Monsters University, everyone had heard the door tech lab alarm go off and was crowded around the lab. While Don distracted the security guards, **Sulley bolted through the door and into the cabin**. He called Mike's name, but the cabin was empty.

Sulley found Mike sitting beside a lake.

"You were right. They weren't scared of me," said the little monster. "I thought I could show everyone that Mike Wazowski is someone special . . . but I'm just not."

Sulley sat down beside Mike. "I'm scary, Mike, but most of the time I'm terrified."

"How come you never told me that before?" asked Mike.

"Because we weren't friends before," replied Sulley.

Just then, the camp rangers arrived. Mike and Sulley ran to the cabin. When they opened the closet door, the monsters were stunned. It was just a closet!

Back in the door tech lab, Hardscrabble had powered down the door. **That meant Mike and Sulley were trapped in the human world!**

Mike had an idea. If they could generate enough scream power, they could activate the door from the human world.

As the rangers crept into the cabin, a fan turned on. The curtains fluttered and the door slammed shut. Claw marks suddenly appeared on the floor. Then the bunk beds toppled over!

Up in the rafters, Mike gave Sulley his cue.

"RAAAAAAAAAAR!" Sulley unleashed his most ferocious roar.

"AHHHHHHHHHHH!" screamed the rangers.

In the lab, Hardscrabble watched as the red light above the door began to pulse.

"Impossible!" she said.

Suddenly, the scream cans on the shelves filled to the brim and shot through the air. **The door began to glow and shake.**

BANG!

Sulley and Mike burst through in a cloud of smoke and debris.

"How . . . how did you do this?" asked Hardscrabble in disbelief.

"Don't ask me," said Sulley, and motioned to Mike.

As Sulley and Mike were escorted out of the lab by security, Hardscrabble was at a loss for words.

Mike and Sulley were expelled from school. They sadly said farewell to Don, Squishy, Art, Terri, and Terry.

"We really messed up," Mike said. "You'd be in the Scaring Program right now if it wasn't for us."

But Hardscrabble had invited the OKs into the program. Mike and Sulley couldn't have been more proud of them.

"So, what now?" Sulley asked Mike at the bus stop.

"For the first time in my life, I don't have a plan," Mike admitted. **"But I'm okay just being okay."**

The two shook hands, and Mike boarded the bus.

It only took a few moments for Sulley to realize he couldn't let Mike leave. He stopped the bus and looked Mike in the eye.

"I don't know a single Scarer who can do what you do," he told Mike. **"You aren't scary, but you are fearless."**

Just then, Dean Hardscrabble appeared. She handed Mike the school newspaper. He and Sulley were on the front page.

"The two of you did something no one has ever done before," said Hardscrabble. **"You surprised me."**

Mike looked at the paper and saw an ad for mail-room workers at Monsters, Inc. He turned to Sulley. "You know what . . . there's still one way I think we can work at a scare floor."

Mike's and Sulley's dreams of working at Monsters, Inc., finally came true! They were determined to be the best mail-room workers ever. It didn't take long before they earned the **"Most Mail Delivered"** award!

Mike and Sulley quickly moved up the ranks of the company. **They soon became the first scare team at Monsters, Inc.!**

On their first day as a team, Mike strode out onto a scare floor.

"You coming, Coach?" asked Sulley.

Mike smiled his biggest smile ever. "You better believe it!"